Thanksgiving at Our House

Thanksgiving at Our House

By P. K. Hallinan

ideals children's books.

Nashville, Tennessee

ISBN-13: 978-0-8249-5654-7

Published by Ideals Children's Books
An imprint of Ideals Publications
A Guideposts Company
Nashville, Tennessee
www.idealsbooks.com

Color separations by Precision Color Graphics, Franklin, Wisconsin

Printed and bound in China

        The Library of Congress has cataloged the hardcover edition as follows:

Hallinan, P. K.
 Thanksgiving at our house / P.K. Hallinan.
    p. cm.
 Summary: Rhyming text reveals the many blessings a child counts on Thanksgiving day.
                    (alk. paper)
[1. Thanksgiving Day—Fiction. 2. Stories in rhyme.] I. Title.
 PZ8.3.H15Tg 2006
 [E]—dc22
                    2006004178

Designed by Georgina Chidlow-Rucker

Reg _ Jun13_1

This book
belongs to

_____

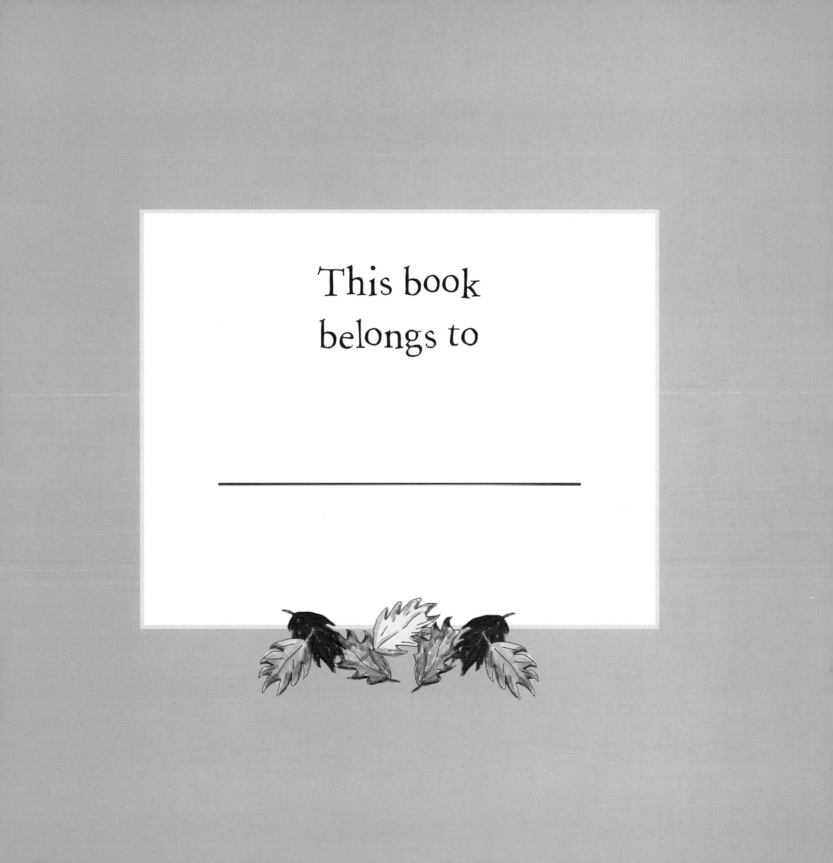

I'm glad for Thanksgiving.
It's a wonderful day
To count all the blessings
That friends bring our way.

First, there's my family.
We're friends, tried and true,

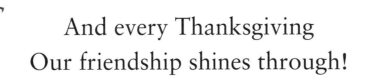

And every Thanksgiving
Our friendship shines through!

We nibble on pancakes
As we watch the parades.

We dress up like Pilgrims
And Indian braves.

And we like to pitch in
With the Thanksgiving meal,
From carrying berries
To carting off peels.

And we keep a close eye
On the whipped cream and pie!

Then come my playmates.
What a wonderful crew
Of happy companions—
And so comical too!

We like to go hiking
In the brisk morning breeze.

We dive into piles
Of colorful leaves.

And sooner or later
We're certain to play
A game of touch football,
Running every which way!

And when we're all done,
We collapse from the fun!

Then, I have neighbors—
My friends on our street.
We usually bring them
Some treats they can eat.

It's warming to see
How they light up and smile

Then invite us inside
To chat for a while.

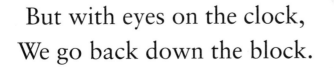

But with eyes on the clock,
We go back down the block.

And soon come my relatives,
Great friends, one and all.
"Happy Thanksgiving!"
We cheerfully call.

Then our living room reels
With hilarious squeals,
Till we race to our places
For the Thanksgiving meal.

And it never is long
Before we break into song!

Later that day,
As we're saying "Goodbye,"
There's one final friend
Who catches my eye.

My trusty dog, Rusty,
Is sitting at my feet,
Impatiently waiting
For a Thanksgiving treat.

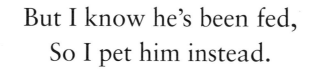

But I know he's been fed,
So I pet him instead.

Yes, Thanksgiving offers
Some wonderful ways
To appreciate friendships
That brighten our days.

So I'm grateful for blessings
That just never end,
But mostly I'm thankful . . .

For family and friends!